THE ROBOBOTS

MATT NOVAK

A DK INK BOOK
DK PUBLISHING, INC.

A Richard Jackson Book

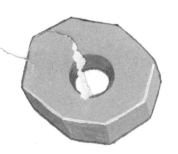

DK Publishing, Inc.
95 Madison Avenue
New York, New York 10016

Visit us on the World Wide Web at http://www.dk.com

Copyright © 1999 by Matt Novak

Library of Congress Cataloging-in-Publication Data

Novak, Matt.
The Robobots / Matt Novak.—1st ed.
p.   cm.

Summary: When the Robobots move onto Littlewood Lane they create controversy with their strange ways, but eventually they convince the neighbors that they are a family worth knowing.

ISBN 0-7894-2566-1
[1. Robots—Fiction.   2. Neighborliness—Fiction.]   I. Title.
PZ7.N867Ri   1998   [E]—dc21   98-7374   CIP   AC

The illustrations for this book were painted in acrylic on watercolor paper.
The text of this book is set in 18 point Triplex Light.
Book design by Liney Li
Printed and bound in U.S.A.

First Edition, 1999
2   4   6   8   10   9   7   5   3   1

To Doug Winner

One day the strangest vehicle anyone had ever seen drove down Littlewood Lane. Mr. Peebles stared in amazement as it stopped in front of the old Wilson house.

The strangest of strange families
stepped out of the vehicle.
"Hello!" they said together. "We are the Robobots."
"I am D.A.D." "I am M.O.M."
"I am Widget." "And I am Toggle."
"You must be our new neighbor."
Mr. Peebles shrieked and ran into his house.
"He must be very shy," said D.A.D.

The Robobots said hello to the mailbox.

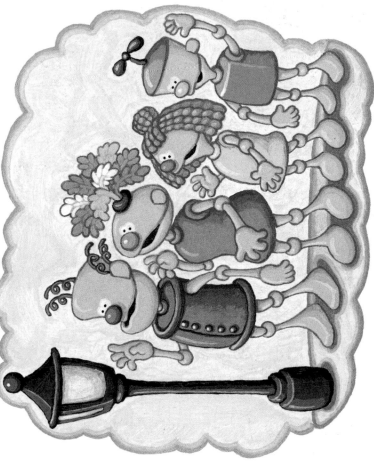

They said hello to the fire hydrant

and hello to the lamppost.
The mailbox, the fire hydrant,
and the lamppost did not say a word.
"Everyone here is very shy," said M.O.M.

"Now we must make ourselves at home," said D.A.D.

"Yes," M.O.M. said. "Then we will be absolutely happy."

"This lawn is the wrong color," said Toggle.

"These trees are the wrong shape," said Widget.

"I must plant the garden," said M.O.M.

"I must fix the house," said D.A.D.

They unloaded the vehicle.

"Kids, be careful with that furniture," M.O.M. warned.

"That is right," said D.A.D. "We do not want to break anyone we know."

When they were all moved in, they stood back
and admired their new home.

"It is a little plain," D.A.D. remarked,
"but we can always add on later."

D.A.D. went to look for a job,
but no one would hire him.
"Perhaps I am dressed wrong," said D.A.D.

M.O.M. went shopping,
but no one would sell her anything.
"Maybe I have the wrong kind of money," said M.O.M.

Widget and Toggle went to school,
but they were not allowed in.
"Maybe it is a holiday," said Toggle.

So the Robobots went back to their house.

"I do not feel at home," sighed Widget.

"I am not absolutely happy," sniffed Toggle.

"Do not cry," said M.O.M. "You will rust."

"Things will work out," said D.A.D.

But over at the Peebles's house, the neighbors had a meeting.

"Their house is ugly!" shouted Mrs. Peebles.

"They talk to mailboxes!" cried Mr. Bumpus.

"They are too different!" yelled Miss Grizwald.

"I think they're from another planet," said Sammy Peebles.

"I think they're from another galaxy," said Betty Peebles.

"Even worse," said Mr. Peebles, "I think they're from the big city."

That really scared everyone.

"They have to go!" shouted Mr. Bumpus.

They all marched over to the Robobots' house
and banged on the door.
"Hello," said the Robobots all together.
"We are the Robobots."
"I am D.A.D." "I am M.O.M."
"I am Widget." "And I am Toggle."
"Yes," said Mr. Peebles. "We already know that."
"Please come in," said D.A.D.
Everyone stepped cautiously inside.

The house was unlike anything they had ever seen.
"My word," said Mr. Bumpus.
"My goodness," said Miss Grizwald.
"My hat!" cried Mr. Peebles as some mechanical creature
ran off with his hat.

"That is just Cousin Coatrack," said M.O.M.

"He is such a practical joker."

The Robobots showed everyone around.

"This is the living room," said D.A.D.

"Wow," said Mr. Peebles. "Where did you get flying furniture?"

"Just a little something I put together," said D.A.D. "I like to build things."

"Me too," said Mr. Peebles. "I bet my boss at the Gizmo Store would like to meet you."

"Wooo-eee! This is fun!" cried Miss Grizwald.

"Here is the kitchen," said M.O.M.

The refrigerator said, "Rink-a-tink-tink. Have a cool drink."

The stove said, "Huff-a-puff-puff. I bake good stuff."

The sink said, "Bub-a-dub-dub. What can I scrub?"

And the garbage can said, "BURP!"

"Wow! What a great kitchen!" exclaimed Mrs. Peebles.

"Yes," said M.O.M. "I love to cook."
"I love to cook too," said Mr. Bumpus.
"Me too," said Mrs. Peebles. "Did you know the market is having a big sale tomorrow?"

The kids played all afternoon in the playroom.
"Wow! These are the best toys I've ever seen," cried Sammy.
"Everyone at school will be amazed," said Betty.

"I thought everyone had toys like these," said Toggle.

"Me too," said Widget.

"Dinnertime!" M.O.M. called.

"I made the cheeseburgers," proclaimed Mr. Bumpus.
"I made the French fries," Mrs. Peebles said proudly.
"This food is very odd," said D.A.D. "But tasty."
And for dessert they all had M.O.M.'s special
chocolate-covered propellers.

Then it was time to go.

Cousin Coatrack gave Mr. Peebles his hat back.

"That is the most fun I've had in years," said Miss Grizwald.

"Me too," said Mr. Bumpus.

"I'll see you at work," said Mr. Peebles.

"I'll see you at the market," said Mrs. Peebles.

"We'll see you at school," said Sammy and Betty.

The Robobots stood at the door and waved.

"Now I really do feel at home," said M.O.M.

"Oh, yes," said Widget and Toggle.

"I agree," said D.A.D.

And the Robobots were absolutely happy. . .

even if some of their neighbors were a little strange.

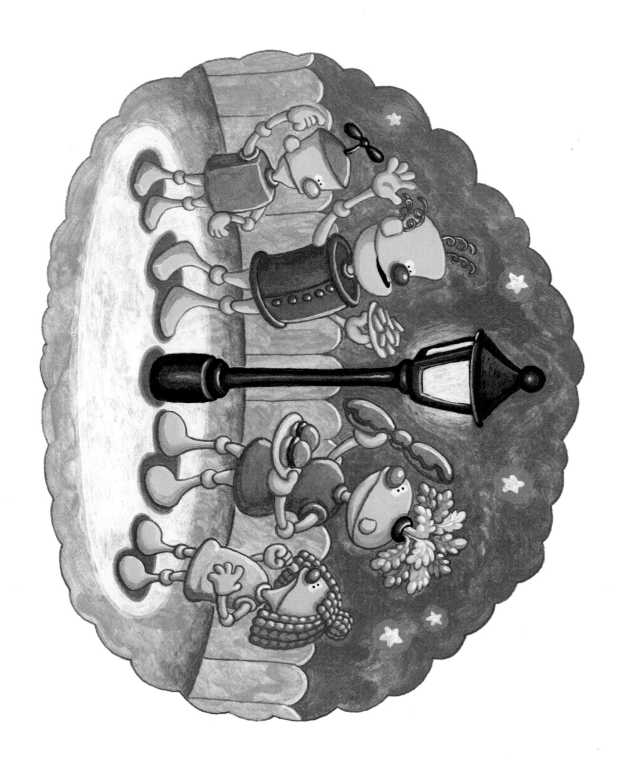

No Dogs Allowed!

by Linda Ashman

illustrated by Kristin Sorra

STERLING CHILDREN'S BOOKS
New York

WELCOME!

Come in, we're OPEN